Shifty McGifty

AND
SLIPPERY SAM

THE DIAMOND CHASE

First published in 2016 by Nosy Crow Ltd
The Crow's Nest, 10a Lant Street
London SE1 1QR
www.nosycrow.com

ISBN 978 0 85763 669 0 (HB)
ISBN 978 0 85763 670 6 (PB)

Nosy Crow and associated logos are trademarks
and/or registered trademarks of Nosy Crow Ltd.

Text copyright © Tracey Corderoy 2016
Illustrations copyright © Steven Lenton 2016

A CIP catalogue record for this book is available from the British Library.

Printed in China by Imago.
Papers used by Nosy Crow are made from wood grown in sustainable forests.

10 9 8 7 6 5 4 3 2 1 (HB)
10 9 8 7 6 5 4 3 2 1 (PB)

For my lovely, lovely Dylan
whose favourite thing is
birthday cake! xx T.C.

For the stupendous
Sarah and Jango x
S.L.

Shifty McGifty
AND
SLIPPERY SAM
THE DIAMOND CHASE

Tracey Corderoy

Illustrated by

Steven Lenton

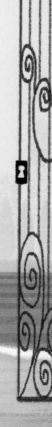

nosy
Crow

Once Shifty and Sam
used to sneak out and rob.
But robbing – they learned – was a terrible job!
So Shifty and Sam chucked their swag bags away.
And now they are bakers, I'm happy to say.

They bake for posh parties in grand houses, too –
where only the **jammiest** doughnuts will do!
"Oh, WOW!" whispered Shifty, as Woofington Hall
was decked out in sparkles for Lady Kate's ball.

She swept down the staircase and there on her head . . .
"Her birthday **tiara**!! Real **diamonds**!" Sam said.
"Come on," Shifty nudged him. "Sam, let's go and bake.
She can't have a birthday without any cake!"

So down in the kitchen, they rolled and they sliced.
They whisked and they whirled – and they patted and iced!

But Lady Kate's nephew just wanted to play.
And Barnaby simply would not go away!
He booted his ball.
"Quick, Sam! Catch it!" he cried.
But Sam gave a squeak.
"Mind the cake!" he replied.

They took up the food to **tremendous** applause.
"Oooh, yummy!" beamed Scottie Dog, rubbing his paws.
He tucked in his napkin, his plate at the ready.
"So one bun for me and – um – one for my teddy!"

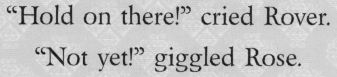

"Hold on there!" cried Rover.
"Not yet!" giggled Rose.
"I think Lady Kate's gone to powder her nose."

They waited, all hoping
she wouldn't be long.
But when she came back . . .

. . . they saw **something** was wrong!
"A thief!" she exclaimed. "At my party!" she sobbed.
"My diamond tiara has gone! I've been ROBBED!"
The whole room fell silent.

"Don't worry," Sam said.
"We've caught thieves before!" Shifty nodded his head.
"You have . . .?" Lady Kate brushed away a big tear.
"Then follow me quickly! Thank goodness you're here!"

She hurried them out to the scene of the crime
and said, "I was fluffing my hair at the time!
My diamond tiara was not on my head.
I'd popped it on one of these statues instead.
But then I turned round, and – quite out of the blue –
the statue had GONE! The tiara had, too!"

WOOFUS
DE
MILO

WOOFSPEARE

WOOFTANIA

"Aha!" nodded Shifty, he narrowed his eyes.
"That statue – I bet – was our thief in disguise!"
"So what did it look like,
this statue?!" Sam cried.
"Just – black, white and . . .
statue-y," Lady Kate sighed.

WOOFHOTEP
III

WOOFPOLEON

"A black and white thief . . . ?"
muttered Shifty. "No WAY!!
I've seen black and white things
around here all day!
Our robber's . . .

. . . a penguin!"

Then who should race by . . .

"That's him! That's the robber!"
Sam said with a cry.

The penguin raced off with a zip and a zoom.
Then – tailcoat a-flapping – dashed into a room!
"Bad move," whispered Shifty.
"Now we've got him trapped!"

"Tee hee!" giggled Sam.
"What a birdbrain!" he clapped.
They followed him in.
There was no need to run . . .

. . . but suddenly Sam gave a squeak!
"Errr, which one?!"
Each penguin – he saw – looked exactly the same.
So *how* would they find out which one was to blame?!

"He's tricked us!" scowled Shifty.
"That robber is trouble."
"Right penguins," said Sam.
"Flippers up – on the double!"
He knew the tiara was not far away.
"We'll find it," said Sam,
"if it takes us all day!"

They searched every waiter.
But then the last one
quite suddenly winked
and broke into a run!
"My name's Sidney Scarper!"
the thief cried with glee.
"And no one – but no one's –
as speedy as me!"

Back out in the hallway, the chase now began –
past presents and bunting, they ran and they **ran**!

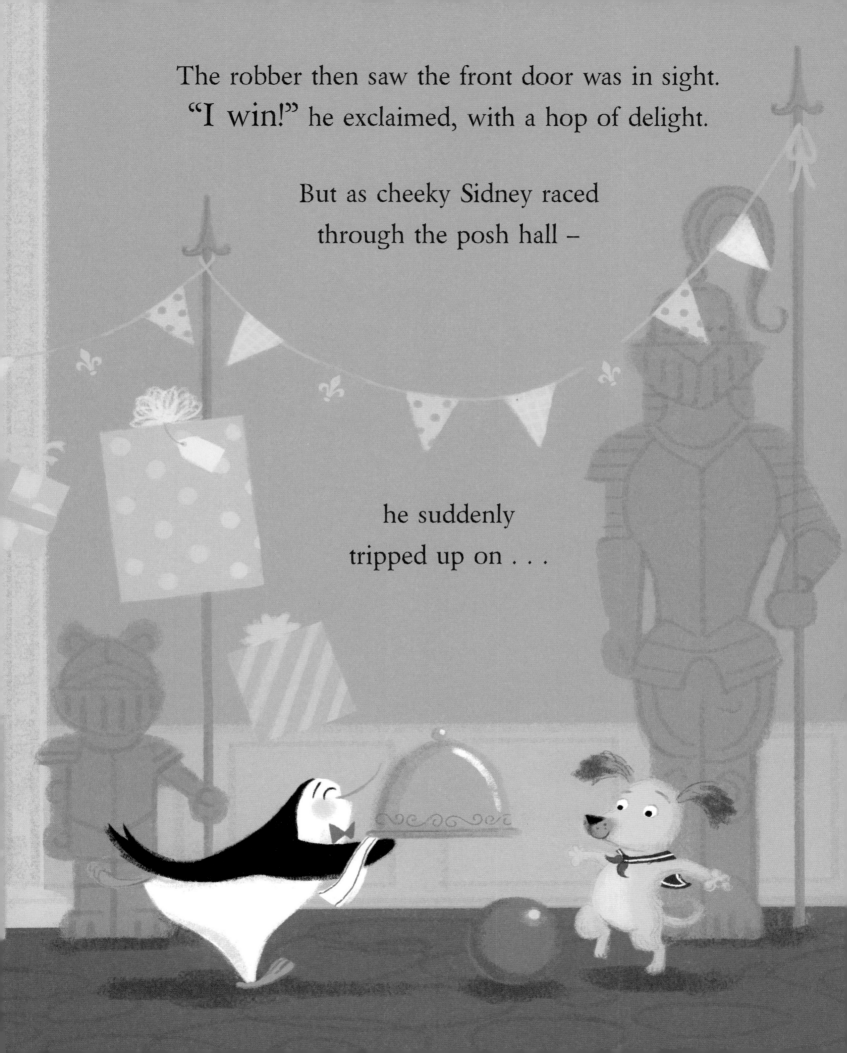

The robber then saw the front door was in sight.
"I win!" he exclaimed, with a hop of delight.

But as cheeky Sidney raced
through the posh hall –

he suddenly
tripped up on . . .

. . . Barnaby's ball!

"Oh NO!" shouted Sidney.
He tumbled and slid.
And what do you think
shot from under his lid . . . ?!

The sparkly tiara flew off through the air.
"Hey, Barnaby – catch it!"
cried Shifty. "Quick! There!"

And everyone gasped
as the pup leaped up high . . .

. . . and **rescued** the jewels
in the blink of an eye!

"Oh, Barnaby!" Lady Kate beamed. "Clever you!"
She thanked Sam and Shifty for helping out, too.

She glared down at Sidney,
who looked very sad.
"I'm *sorry . . .*" he sniffled.
"I've been . . . really . . . bad.
I *shouldn't* have robbed you.
It's WRONG, now I see.
Besides, the tiara
looked rubbish on me!"

"You promise," Sam nodded,
"you'll make a new start?"
"I promise you!" Sidney cried,
flipper on heart.

And then, to make up
for the **bad** thing he'd done . . .

. . . he piled up the dishes and washed EVERY one!